The Chocolate
TOUCH

**If you enjoy reading this book, you might like
to try another story from the**

MAMMOTH READ

series:

The Chocolate
TOUCH

Patrick Skene Catling

Illustrated by Glenys Ambrus

mammoth

First published in the USA
by William Morrow & Company Inc
First published in Great Britain 1984
by Methuen Children's Books Ltd
This edition first published 1990 by Mammoth
Reissued 2000 by Mammoth
an imprint of Egmont Children's Books Limited
239 Kensington High Street, London W8 6SA

ISBN 0 7497 0306 7

10 9 8 7

A CIP catalogue record for this title
is available from the British Library

Printed in Great Britain
by Cox & Wyman Ltd, Reading, Berkshire

For Sheila, Ellen, Charlotte and Desmond –
and for Iris Diana

One

Most of the time John Midas was really quite a nice boy. Every now and then, of course, he broke a rule, such as the rule against pretending to be a girl-eating tiger when his younger sister, Mary, was supposed to be getting to sleep.

In most respects, he was healthy, normal and average, or sometimes, on a good day, slightly above average. He was tall enough but not too tall. He wasn't fat and he wasn't skinny. He was lean, with some muscles that were beginning to show. His hair was medium-brown and of medium length, his eyes were sort of greenish and his face was pleasantly ordinary, except, of course, when he twisted it into monstrous shapes, just for fun, or because he was in an awful mood.

John Midas lived in a comfortable house in a quiet street in Hampstead Garden Suburb, near the playing fields below Hampstead Heath, in London. There were plenty

of trees in the Heath and bushes to hide
behind and chase round.

John's mother was gentle as well as prac-
tical. She was a good cook. His father, when
he didn't have to rush to catch the Under-
ground, was generally cheerful. On fine
weekends he often took John and Mary for
walks and told them interesting things about

beetles, birds' nests, brigands and but-
terflies.

John went to a local school and usually
liked it. His teacher that year was Miss
Plimsole, who wasn't really as strict as she
pretended. She was fairly easy to get along
with when he did careful work. He had
received a new, shiny golden trumpet as a
going-to-school present. Mrs Quaver, the
music teacher, had soon agreed to let him
play small parts, a few notes at a time, with
the school orchestra.

And there was Susan Buttercup, who was in his class. Susan had yellow curls, pink cheeks, blue eyes, and one of the best collections of marbles in the neighbourhood.

John should have been absolutely all right. But he wasn't.

He had one bad fault: he was a pig about sweets. Toffees, lollipops, licorice all-sorts, fruit pastilles, peppermint rock, old-fashioned bulls' eyes, Turkish delight, fudge, black-currant lozenges for ticklish throats, nougat, acid-drops, *marrons glacés*, marshmallows, and, first and last, above all, chocolates—he devoured them all.

While other children spent their pocket-money on model spaceships, comics, skipping ropes, tropical fish and other useful

things, John studied the sweet counters. All his money went on sweets, and all his sweets went to himself. He never shared them. John Midas was mad about sweets.

At lunch one Saturday Mrs Midas noticed a few little red spots on the end of John's nose.

'Look,' she said to Mr Midas, in a told-you-so tone of voice. 'John has spots.'

Mr Midas leaned forward to look at them. He gravely shook his head and clicked his tongue.

John tried to look too. But it is impossible to see the very tip of your own nose without a mirror, unless you happen to be an elephant with a long nose that you can bend double.

When John tried to examine the end of his nose, first with one eye and then with the other, and then with both together, all that he could see was a pink blur. Looking at something so close made his eyes ache.

'I can't see any spots, Mummy,' John said.

'Well, I can,' Mr Midas said. 'Just because you don't see something doesn't always mean it isn't there. Feel the end of your nose with a finger.'

John rubbed his nose. It did feel a bit rough.

'It may be measles,' Mrs Midas said anxiously. She placed a tender hand on John's forehead to feel whether it was warmer than usual. 'But I don't think he has a temperature.'

'He's already had measles,' Mr Midas reminded her. 'I suspect John's been eating too many sweets again. Have you been eating sweets this morning, John?'

'Some,' John reluctantly admitted.

'What?' Mr Midas asked.

'Well,' John replied. 'I had a few Cream Delights. Susan gave them to me. I gave her my rubber frog, the one that was in my Christmas stocking.'

With an impatient hand, Mr Midas brushed aside John's account of the day's swapping.

'Anything else?' Mr Midas demanded.

'A little Toffee Crunch,' John said.

'And what else?' Mr Midas asked, beginning to look cross.

John's ears reddened. He knew he wasn't supposed to eat sweets before meals.

'Oh,' he said. 'Only, er, oh . . . hardly anything else.'

'John!' Mr Midas exclaimed, and John recognized the expression on his father's face. It meant that John had to tell everything, without any further delay.

It turned out that John had been to see most of his friends and had managed to get sweets from nearly all of them. The list he recited was a long one.

'No wonder you have spots,' Mr Midas commented at last. He sighed. 'I think we'd better take John to see Dr Cranium,' he said to Mrs Midas.

Dr Cranium was a tall, thin man with a bald head and a grey moustache. He looked through his glasses at John and said, 'Hmmm.'

'He eats a lot of sweets,' Mr Midas said.
'He hasn't been eating his meals properly,' Mrs Midas said.
'That's just what I thought,' Dr Cranium said. 'I can tell by looking at him that he eats far too many sweets.'

9

The doctor shone a little electric torch into John's right ear. Then he shone it into John's left ear. Then he shone it up into John's right nostril. He told John to open his mouth wide and to say 'Ah'. Then the doctor shone the torch into John's mouth.

'Far too many sweets!' Dr Cranium protested. 'Gracious me! The boy seems to be full of sweets!'

He told John to sit back and relax. Then the doctor picked up a small rubber-headed hammer and gave John a light tap on the right knee, just below the joint. John's foot gave a weak kick. John giggled.

'It's nothing to laugh about,' Mr Midas said.

'No, John,' the doctor said reprovingly. 'A healthy little boy who didn't eat too many sweets would kick harder than that.'

'I'm sorry,' John said politely, 'but I can kick harder if you want me to.' He gave a sudden high kick, like a goalkeeper's, which knocked the hammer out of Dr Cranium's hand. The hammer landed on its rubber head and bounced across the room.

'John!' exclaimed Mrs Midas. 'I'm so sorry, Dr Cranium. John, tell Dr Cranium you're sorry for kicking his hammer.'

'I'm sorry I kicked your hammer,' John said, pressing his lips together to prevent them from smiling.

'I would recommend fewer sweets,' Dr Cranium rather crossly told Mr and Mrs Midas. 'An upset stomach can lead to all sorts of complications.'

On the way home Mrs Midas tried to explain to John what she thought the doctor had meant by complications.

'You see,' she said patiently, 'if you put too much of one kind of food into your stomach and not enough of other kinds, it's bad for your whole body, because different parts of your body need different kinds of food. Do you understand?'

'I think so,' John said. He felt restless. Sometimes his parents' explanations were rather boring.

'You have been eating so much sweet stuff,' Mr Midas said, 'that there isn't any room for meat and vegetables and eggs and bread and milk and apples and fish and bananas and . . . all the other things you're supposed to have to make you grow big and strong.'

'I like bananas,' John said. 'Especially in thin slices covered with chocolate. They're called Banana Surprises.'

Mr Midas looked at Mrs Midas, and Mrs Midas looked at Mr Midas. They both shrugged their shoulders. Sometimes it was hard to make John understand.

At home, while Mrs Midas was busy in the kitchen, Mr Midas continued to reason with John.

'You mean you'd rather eat sweets than anything else, and chocolate rather than any other kind of sweets?' Mr Midas asked.

'Yes!' John assured him. 'Oh, yes!'

'Don't you think there's such a thing as enough?' Mr Midas grimly persisted. 'Don't you think that things are best in their places? I mean, don't you think there's time for spaghetti and a time for roast beef and even a time for pickled herring and garlic toast, as well as a time for chocolate? Or would you rather have chocolate all the time?'

'Chocolate all the time,' John replied emphatically. 'Chocolate's best, that's all. Other things are just food. But chocolate's chocolate. Chocolate –'

'All right,' Mr Midas interrupted sharply. He took a deep breath and went on. 'Very well. John, if you can't understand what sort of diet is really best for you, can't you at least get it into your head that you make your mother very unhappy when you eat so many sweets that you can't eat anything else?'

Here we go again, John thought. The conversation always seemed to get around to the effect of John's eating sweets on John's mother. John couldn't see how it could possibly do her any harm if he ate sweets. He sat silent for a moment. Then he said: 'May I go out and play, please, Daddy?'

Two

It was Sunday afternoon. The sun was sinking low in the sky, but the air was still quite warm. John was wandering along in the direction of Susan's house, absentmindedly looking down at the pavement for odds and ends to kick, when his eye was suddenly caught by a dully gleaming, silver-grey coin lying right in his path.

The coin was the size of a 10p piece. But even as he eagerly leaned down to pick it up, John noticed there was something strange about it. There was no picture of Queen Elizabeth II or a lion with a crown on its head. On one side of the coin there was a picture of a boy with round cheeks, and on the other side there was nothing but the letters J M – which was funny, John thought, because those letters happened to be his own initials.

Grasping the coin firmly, he ran on towards Susan's house. She liked collecting things. He thought she might be interested

to know that he had the beginning of a coin collection.

Although he was in the habit of going over to Susan's by the same route once or twice almost every day, this afternoon John found himself turning left where he usually turned right.

I always go the same way, he thought. This time, for a change, I'm going a new way. John was the sort of person who likes to experiment. He did not stop to consider that you cannot go east by going west, unless you go all the way around the world.

Only a short distance along the unfamiliar street, John came to a small corner shop. It was a neat, new building with two show windows. They both contained elaborate displays of sweets. Susan was immediately forgotten.

John pressed his nose against one of the windows. He was imagining the taste of chocolate-covered almonds and chocolate fudge on the other side of the glass when he noticed a white-haired old man wearing a white apron, leaning against the counter, beckoning to him. John was surprised when the man called him by name. John had never been there before.

'Come in, John!' the man said. 'Don't stand out there. Come and get some fresh, sweet, creamy chocolate. There's a special sale today.'

The shopkeeper saw John hesitate.

'The chocolate I use in my kitchen comes direct from the heart of Africa. Sugar from

16

Jamaica, butter and cream from Devon . . . I use only the finest ingredients. And my recipes! You've never had chocolates like mine before. Come in!'

'Thank you,' John replied, walking to the counter. He was fascinated. 'But, you see, the trouble is . . . well . . . '

'No money?' the shopkeeper suggested with a sympathetic smile. 'No money whatsoever? What've you got there in your hand?'

John had forgotten the old coin he had just found.

'Oh,' he said, 'this is part of my coin collection. I mean,' he added more honestly, 'I'm going to save this coin and then get some more to make a collection.'

'Let me have a look at it,' the shopkeeper said. He looked briefly at the coin. 'Aha!' he exclaimed.

'Is it any good?' John asked, his hopes rising.

'Very good,' said the shopkeeper. 'In fact, it's the only kind of money I accept. But I don't suppose you'd want to spend it on a box—'

'A whole box?'

'I imagine you'd rather keep this for your coin collection than spend it on chocolate, wouldn't you?'

'Oh, no!' John assured him. 'Chocolate any day!'

'Go ahead then,' the old man said. 'Help yourself.' He pointed to a show table piled high with large boxes, all wrapped in shiny gold and purple Cellophane, all exactly alike.

'I can have one of *those*?' John asked, his eyes round with surprise. The chocolate boxes were as big as the ones his father brought home for the whole family to share

18

at Christmas time.

'Just help yourself,' the shopkeeper repeated. 'That is, unless you think it might be better to ask your mother first.'

'She wouldn't mind,' John said hastily, and blushed. He did not *like* telling lies, and usually tried not to.

The shopkeeper winked knowingly.

'I'm sure she won't,' he agreed. 'Not in the long run, anyway.'

John tucked one of the large boxes under his arm, declined the shopkeeper's offer to wrap the box as a gift, thanked him, and hurried out of the shop before there could be any question of anybody's changing his mind.

The shopkeeper smiled thoughtfully as he watched his customer running back the way he had come.

John decided that it might be sensible to enter his house quietly by way of the kitchen. With the large box hidden behind him, he let himself in by the back door and crept up the kitchen stairs on tiptoe towards his own room on the top floor. Just as he was about to turn the corner on the first floor landing to continue his way upstairs, he had to stop, hiding for a moment while his father walked by, coming from the bedroom telephone.

'That was Mrs Buttercup on the telephone,' Mr Midas called to Mrs Midas, as he walked down the front stairs. 'She said she was sorry John hadn't been able to get over to play with Susan this afternoon. But it was a good thing in a way, she thought, because Susan's already so excited about her birthday party tomorrow. I wonder where John can have got to.'

As soon as the first floor was quiet again and John knew there was no danger that his chocolate box would be seen, he hurried silently up to his bedroom, pushed open the door, and slid the box under the bed. Then he walked heavily down the front stairs to the living room.

'Well, there you are,' said Mrs Midas.'We couldn't imagine where you were. What've you been doing?"

'Oh, just sort of playing about,' John said.

John usually took a long time to put his things away and undress and have his bath and get ready for bed, for he thought sleeping was a waste of time. But this evening he started yawning long before his customary bedtime.

'Ho, hum. Ho-o-o, hummm. Sleepy,' he announced.

'All right,' said Mrs Midas. 'Time for your tonic.'

Dr Cranium had prescribed a large bottle of tonic for John. The thick liquid was dark brown, with a green glint, like motor oil. John had to drink a tablespoonful of it every night to make up for all the vegetables and fruit that he left on his plates at lunch and dinner. The tonic tasted like soap, glue, ink and paint. It tasted like the worst mixture you can imagine.

Much to Mrs Midas's surprise, John ran ahead of her to the dining-room cupboard where the tonic and the tonic spoon were kept. By the time she got there he had already filled the spoon. Then, without any coaxing, he emptied it into his mouth and

swallowed it.

'Ugh!' John spluttered. 'Oof! Baw!'

'That's a very good boy,' Mrs Midas said. 'Now why can't you eat up your dinner that way? If only you'd stop eating so many sweets you wouldn't need to take that tonic.'

Soon John was scrubbed and in his pyjamas and in bed, ready to be tucked in for the night. Mrs Midas sat on the edge of the

bed and stroked his forehead for a moment.
Then she kissed his cheek. John, pretending
that he was very sleepy, shut his eyes and
began breathing deeply.

When Mrs Midas rejoined Mr Midas in
the living room, she said: 'I've never known
John to be so good about going to bed. He
went to sleep in no time.'

A few seconds after the bedroom door had
closed behind his mother, John leaped to the
floor, got down on his hands and knees, and
felt under the bed for the chocolate box. He
soon had it on the pillow and set to work
unfastening it. First he took off the thin outer

sheet of Cellophane. Then he lifted off the lid. Then he removed a sheet of cardboard. Then he pulled off a sheet of heavy silver tin-foil. Then he took out a thick layer of shredded paper.

As the wrappings piled up around him, John became rather anxious. At last he came to a small central ball of cotton wool, and there, right in the middle, was a little golden ball. He picked at it with his fingernail and peeled away the gold paper, revealing a tiny ball of plain chocolate. It was the only piece of chocolate in the whole box.

John was deeply disappointed. He felt that he had been cheated. Even so, he put the piece of chocolate into his mouth. It began to melt on his tongue. He had never before tasted a chocolate quite like it. It was the most chocolatey chocolate he had ever eaten.

Three

The birds were chirping in the tree outside John's window, and the sky beyond was blue. The bedroom door opened a few inches.

'Hey, sleepy!' Mrs Midas called. 'Everyone else is up!'

John put on his dressing-gown and slippers and ambled to the bathroom. His sister, Mary, was still brushing her teeth, and he had to wait until she finished.

'Come on, Mary,' he said impatiently. 'Don't take all morning.'

'Here you are,' she said, handing him the toothpaste tube.

While Mary washed her face, John squeezed a little of the toothpaste onto his brush. The paste was pink. John made a face at his toothbrush. It didn't seem fair that he had to brush his teeth with stuff that tasted like his tonic. 'A stinky taste,' he called it.

He opened his mouth and pushed in the end of the toothbrush. As soon as it touched

his front teeth he noticed a delicious sweet-
ness in his mouth, a taste of the best chocolate. He pushed the brush to and fro, and the
taste grew stronger. He removed the toothbrush. The bristles were brown.

'What kind of toothpaste is this?' John
asked.

Mary was drying her face.

'The same kind,' she answered. 'It says on
the tube.'

'*Blanco-Dent*,' John read. It was the kind
they had always had.

'Why is it chocolate-flavoured this time?'
he asked. 'Boy, it's good!'

'Don't be silly!' Mary said. 'Course it isn't
chocolate-flavoured!'

She hung up her towel and swished out of
the bathroom.

John squeezed some more toothpaste onto
his brush and continued to brush his teeth.
Chocolate again! It was wonderful – rich,
sweet, smooth chocolate, chocolatey chocolate, like the piece of chocolate from the box
the night before.

There seemed to be no further need for the
toothbrush, so John rinsed it and hung it up.
He squeezed out another inch of toothpaste,
onto a fingertip. He put his finger in his

mouth and ate the toothpaste off. When he
took his finger out, it was stained chocolate
brown. John wasted no time. He put the end
of the toothbrush tube into his mouth and
emptied the paste onto his tongue. It
squeezed out in his mouth like thick, creamy
chocolate.

Mary looked into the bathroom.

'Hey, what are you doing?' she asked
suspiciously.

'Yummy!' was all John said, with a big
grin.

John and Mary were a bit late getting to the dining room, and Mr Midas was already on the way to his train when they sat down to breakfast.

'John ate up all the toothpaste,' Mary told their mother.

'Ooh, you rotten sneak!' John whispered.

'Well, you did,' Mary reminded him. 'And that's a waste. Isn't it a waste, Mummy, eating up all the toothpaste in one day?'

Mrs Midas was serving their orange juice.

'Mary!' she protested. 'Really! I'm sure John was only joking. He must have been pretending to eat the toothpaste.'

'No, he wasn't,' Mary insisted. 'I was watching, and I saw him squeeze it right into his mouth. He said it was chocolate.'

'Oh, dear,' said Mrs Midas. 'Chocolate again! Now I know he was joking. He just wished it were chocolate, Mary. Come on now, drink up your orange juice, both of you. Your bacon and eggs will be ready in a minute. You mustn't be late for school.'

As Mrs Midas left the room, John took up his glass of orange juice and put it to his lips. As soon as he tilted it and the liquid began to flow into his mouth, a happy look came into his eyes.

'Gosh, that's good!' he said at last, lowering the empty glass. 'Chocolate juice.'

Mary looked at John. Then she looked at her glass of orange juice. It was a bright orange colour. She tasted it. It tasted of oranges.

'It's *not* chocolate juice,' she said. 'It's orange juice. Orange juice is good for you.'

'Yes, John,' Mrs Midas said, hearing the last few words as she re-entered the room, carrying in the plates of bacon and eggs. 'You must drink your –' She saw John's empty glass. 'Why, John! What a good boy! That's the first time for ages you've finished your orange juice without having to be persuaded.'

'It tasted of chocolate,' John explained simply.

'All right,' Mrs Midas said. 'Very funny. But don't tease Mary too much. Remember, she's younger than you.'

John silently picked up his knife and fork and sliced the yoke of a fried egg. The yellow broke over the white and he shivered in disgust as he watched it glop all over the plate.

'I can't eat this,' he told his mother, as he always did.

29

'Of course you can,' Mrs Midas said encouragingly. 'You drank your orange juice. You can eat your bacon and eggs.'

John scraped up a small piece of egg and cautiously put it into his mouth. It immediately turned into chocolate – chocolate white and chocolate yolk. Both lovely, lovely chocolate.

'Mmm!' John mumbled. 'Chocolate egg! Just like Easter.'

In next to no time, he finished every scrap of egg on his plate. Then he tried the bacon. The bacon also turned into chocolate.

John had never before enjoyed his breakfast so much. After the orange juice that had turned into chocolate juice in his mouth and the fried bacon and eggs that had turned into fried chocolate, he ate two slices of chocolate toast with chocolate butter and chocolate marmalade, washed down with a glass of chocolate milk.

'I'm very pleased with you this morning,' Mrs Midas said, as she helped John on with his coat. 'If you promise to eat your lunch at school as well as you ate your breakfast I'll give you some money to buy sweets with.'

'Oh, it's all right,' John said mysteriously. 'I don't think I'll need it.'

Mrs Midas looked very puzzled as she waved goodbye.

Four

John had the bad habit of chewing things when he was thinking hard. This morning he had several things to think about. What had made the toothpaste taste like chocolate? What had made the orange juice, the bacon and eggs, the toast and butter and marmalade taste like chocolate?

Each one of these things had felt the way it had always felt before. The toothpaste had been soft and smooth; the bacon had been hot, crisp, and oily, and the eggs had been slippery and runny; and the toast had been crunchy and the marmalade sticky and lumpy. But everything had tasted like the chocolate he had eaten in bed the night before.

He put a gloved thumb in his mouth and thoughtfully chewed. His mother had frequently pointed out that when he chewed his gloves he made little holes in them that let in the cold air. But he chewed them just the same when he was thinking hard.

This time he noticed something very odd about the thumb of his glove. Instead of tasting leathery, it tasted like chocolate. He pulled his thumb out of his mouth. The part of the glove that had been in his mouth was now brown, instead of black like the rest.

He bit the end of the leather thumb again. It came right off in his mouth, leaving his own thumb bare. John chewed, and it was like chewing leather made of chocolate, leather that melted like chocolate . . . . In a few seconds he swallowed it.

The gloves were not new. John had had them for quite some time. He couldn't think why he had never before thought of eating them. He tried to tear off one of the fingers but the leather was too strong to do that. He put it into his mouth; the leather immediately turned into chocolate, and he was able to break it off easily. He popped it into his mouth and chewed it up and swallowed it. Delicious!

Walking along devouring his glove, John did not notice one of his schoolfellows, Spider Wilson, until he heard his voice.

'John's gone crazy! John's gone crazy!' Spider yelled. Then he turned to John.

'Don't they feed you where you live?'

33

Spider sneered. He was in the form just above John's and was one of the nastiest boys in the whole school.

John gulped down a large piece of the second glove's palm and looked pleased.

'What's the matter with you?' Spider demanded. 'Do your people make you eat leather?'

'This is special leather,' John replied. He licked his lips and sighed contentedly. 'It turns into chocolate as soon as you put it into your mouth. Look.'

He bit off the glove's little finger and took it out of his mouth.

'See? Now it's chocolate.' He put it back into his mouth and swallowed it.

'Give me a piece,' Spider said.

'Why should I?' John asked. 'They're my gloves.'

'*Hand over a piece*,' Spider said emphatically. He was bigger than John and famous for bullying.

'Do I eat your gloves?' John asked reasonably, his mouth full of chocolate. 'Why should you eat mine?'

'Those aren't real gloves,' Spider said. 'Whenever one person has some sweets he has to share them with the others. That's the club rule.'

'What club?' John asked.

'Never mind what club,' Spider said impatiently. 'You'd better let me have some of that chocolate.'

Without waiting any longer, Spider snatched what was left of the second glove. John was too surprised to resist, and he didn't really want to, anyhow. He had a feeling that he had had enough chocolate for a while. He was getting a bit thirsty.

Spider ran only a little way ahead. When he saw that John wasn't going to fight to get the glove back, Spider started to eat his prize. He stuffed the leather into his mouth and took a big bite. Then he stopped short in his tracks. He frowned and again bit deep into the leather. Disgusting! It tasted worse than plain leather. It tasted of leather with which a boy had made innumerable mud

pies and snowballs and had patted old dogs.

John thought perhaps he might be getting late for school, so he started running. He left Spider Wilson spitting the soggy remains of the glove into the gutter.

Still giggling to himself about the defeat of his enemy, John walked between the great stone pillars at the entrance to the school grounds. He had gone no more than half-way to the main building when he heard Susan Buttercup calling him. She was standing near the swings and the slide with some of her friends.

'I've got something to show you, John!' she shouted.

As she came running to meet him, he could see that she was waving something in her hand that flashed as it reflected the rays of the sun. It was a crown piece commemorating the wedding of the Prince and Princess of Wales.

'It's a birthday present,' Susan said. 'Isn't it beautiful? There's a special case to keep it in.'

The sight of such wealth made John forget for a moment the triumphs of his own day.

'It's a good present,' he acknowledged. 'Are you sure it's made of silver, though? I once got a whole bag of gold coins in a Christmas stocking, only they were chocolate coins covered with gold paper.'

'Of course it's real, silly,' Susan said. 'My daddy said so. You can feel it if you don't believe me.' She handed him the coin. 'Bite it, if you think it isn't real. Go on, bite it!'

John felt rather embarrassed.

'I can see it's real now,' he said. 'There's no need for me to bite it.'

'But I want you to,' Susan insisted. 'You weren't sure. Well, *make* sure. That's what they do on television. When a cowboy wants to make sure a silver dollar's real he bites it.'

John put the coin about half-way into his mouth and bit it. His teeth went right through the coin. The part that had passed between his lips was hard, sweet chocolate.

Susan could hardly believe her eyes. She had given John a complete circle of silver. He sadly handed back a crescent.

He did not know what to say. She couldn't speak. Tears trickled down her cheeks like rain down a windowpane. She looked at the piece of coin in her hand. She looked up at John, whose face was red with anguish.

'John Midas,' she blurted out at last, 'I hate you.'

She turned and ran away before he could
think of anything to say to her.

Five

John hung up his coat, got his notebook and pencil out of his locker, and sat down at his small table just in time for the second bell, when Miss Plimsole walked silently into the classroom. As soon as she appeared in the doorway, all the chattering and scuffling stopped. The twenty boys and girls sat straight in their chairs and looked straight ahead at the clean blackboard.

'Good morning, children,' Miss Plimsole said.

'Good morning, Miss Plimsole,' the class responded.

Miss Plimsole sat at her desk, blinking her eyes as she surveyed the room. Then she opened a little drawer in her desk and produced a spectacle case, from which she took her reading glasses. She removed her long-distance glasses, put on her short-distance glasses, snapped shut the spectacle case, replaced it in the drawer, shut the drawer, tilted her head forward so that she could look over the glasses on her nose, and said: 'This morning, children, we are going to have an important test.'

There were some groans and a few 'ooh's' and 'ah's'. (There are children who actually like tests.)

Miss Plimsole lifted one of her hands, and silence was instantly restored.

'No complaining, please!' she said. 'This test will show me how well you have been learning your arithmetic so far this year. It will be a short one. I am going to write four problems on the board. I shall expect you to solve them swiftly and accurately and to write down your answers neatly. You will place your paper in front of you now. You will write your name at the top right-hand corner. And then you will place your pencil beside your paper, sit back in your chair, and wait until I give the signal to begin work.'

Miss Plimsole turned to the blackboard and began chalking up the test problems.

Tests always made John nervous. Besides, his lips were feeling dry, and the taste of chocolate was strong in his mouth. He raised his hand and coughed.

'Yes, John?' Miss Plimsole asked.

'Please may I go and get a drink of water, please, Miss Plimsole?' he asked in a meek voice.

'Very well. Hurry back. We're going to start in a few minutes.'

John gratefully slipped out of the room and walked quickly down the quiet corridor to a water-fountain. His tongue felt thick with chocolate. The cold water would be refreshing.

He pressed his foot down on the fountain treadle, and a stream of clear, ice-cold water spurted up from the silver nozzle in the white enamel basin. He lowered his head until the jet of water reached his lips. The cold water splashed delightfully against the outside of his mouth. He opened his lips. As soon as the water gushed in, it turned into ice-cold chocolate-water, thin and sweet.

Quickly stopping the flow, John looked with dismay at the shallow puddle that had formed and was now draining away in the basin. He hurried to another fountain, on the first floor. But there the same thing happened. The clear, ice-cold water turned to liquid chocolate in his mouth.

When John finally got back to his classroom, all the other pupils were bent over their tables, busily writing. Miss Plimsole looked up from her book as John tiptoed in. She looked at the clock on the wall, looked back at him, and reprovingly wagged her finger.

John began on the first of the four problems, but he was so upset by the chocolate-water that he could not keep his mind on his work. By the time he was ready to start the fourth problem, the other boys and girls were already putting down their pencils and straightening up and smiling at each other. It had not been a very difficult test.

'Two minutes to go,' said Miss Plimsole.

Concentrating hard, John took the end of his pencil between his teeth and began to nibble it. It immediately turned into chocolate. Then he noticed an even more disturbing change. Although he had taken the pencil out of his mouth as soon as the first piece of chocolate had crumbled off, the pencil was continuing to change into chocolate. The chocolate was slowly, steadily moving down the pencil, replacing the wood and the lead inside, changing it into a chocolate pencil before his very eyes. The magic — for John now knew that his power must be

44

some sort of magic – was apparently becoming stronger.

By the time the whole pencil had changed from red, pale yellow and black to dark brown, Miss Plimsole was announcing that only a few seconds remained in which to write down the final answer.

'Just a minute!' John pleaded.

'Sh!' Miss Plimsole cautioned him, holding a finger up against her mouth.

'Sh!' chorused the slow workers, who were becoming almost as agitated as John. But John felt worst of all. He felt sure that he could finish the problem and write down the correct answer, if only he had something to write with.

'But Miss Plimsole,' he begged in a loud whisper, 'my pencil's turned into chocolate!'

'*Hush*, John!' Miss Plimsole said. 'I'll speak to you after the bell.'

John tried to write with his changed pencil. But the point was too soft, and where he meant to write 72 he managed to make only a chocolate smear.

Six

When the others had been excused to go out for midmorning play, John had to go and stand by Miss Plimsole's desk.

'John,' Miss Plimsole said, 'You mustn't make up silly stories to excuse your failures. I must have the truth. What did you do with your pencil?'

'This is it,' he said giving his teacher the pointed stick of chocolate. 'Really it is. It's changed.'

'What do you mean, it's *changed*?' Miss Plimsole demanded.

'That is my pencil,' John tried to explain, 'only it isn't the same any more. Nothing stays the same today if I put it into my mouth. The same thing happened when I chewed my gloves. They turned into chocolate, too.'

'John,' Miss Plimsole said slowly, 'do . . . you . . . feel . . . all . . . right?'

'Yes, thank you,' John said. 'Except ,' he

added, 'I'm getting so thirsty. The water from the drinking fountain turned into chocolate and so did the water from the fountain upstairs. I *would* like a drink of cold water.'

'Yes, John,' Miss Pimsole said. She suddenly looked pale. 'You'd better run out and play with the others. I'm going to have a talk with the nurse. And John,' she said, as he started towards the classroom door, 'here's another pencil. Be a good boy and try not to lose it. I'm afraid I'll have to keep this piece of chocolate until after school. You know we never allow anyone to eat sweets in class.'

Miss Plimsole put the slightly chewed chocolate pencil in her desk drawer. John went out to look for Susan. He found her with two other girls, skipping.

John usually scorned skipping. He preferred hide-and-seek, space wars, or any other good, exciting game. Jumping up and down in one place to avoid being hit by a rope seemed to him to be a waste of time. But he was very sorry to have spoiled Susan's coin and he was willing to make a sacrifice.

'Susan,' he said.

Susan continued to bounce on one foot as her two friends swung the rope, over and

under, over and under, over and under her. She didn't seem to see John.

'I'll skip with you,' he offered.

Susan stopped, and the rope was caught by her shins.

'Let's try doubles, backwards,' she said, but not to John. She ignored him. 'You go first, Sheila. Ellen, you go second. I'll go last. The one who does it most times gets the first slice of my birthday cake.'

Susan looked at John, raised her eyebrows, shut her eyes, and stuck out the tip of her pink tongue. Then she turned back to the girls and smiled. Ellen whispered into Sheila's ear, and Sheila whispered into Susan's. Then all three of them looked at John and at each other again and burst out laughing in a secret way.

'Oh, Susan!' John protested. 'I didn't mean to do it. The trouble is there's something magic about me today. Everything I put into my mouth turns into chocolate.'

The girls hooted with laughter.

'It isn't funny,' John said. 'You wouldn't like it.' He was beginning to feel sorry for himself. 'I think it's getting worse,' he added reproachfully. 'At first just the part in my mouth turned into chocolate, but when I nibbled the end of my pencil the whole pencil changed.'

'Pooh!' was Susan's only comment, and the others hooted with glee.

'Maybe I'll get sick and die,' John warned. 'Maybe I'll turn into chocolate myself. Then you'll be sorry.'

'I don't believe one word about the chocolate,' Susan said. 'And if it was true, you'd be glad, because all you ever like eating is chocolate.'

'If you don't believe me,' John retorted indignantly, 'just give me that skipping rope and I'll prove it.'

The girls looked at each other questioningly for an instant. But as they hesitated the bell rang, and it was time to go back to the classroom.

The rest of the morning passed slowly for John. He was afraid that his mother was going to be cross about the missing gloves. She might not accept the excuse that he had eaten them. He regretted his messed-up arithmetic test. He was sad about Susan's anger and disbelief. And he was getting really terribly thirsty. Once during Reading and once during Art he was allowed to go to get a drink of water. Both times, however, he swallowed nothing but sweet chocolate. His mouth was getting sweeter and stickier and drier by the minute.

Seven

'All right, boys and girls,' Miss Plimsole said brightly. 'It's almost time for lunch. Clear up your things: paint pots securely closed, brushes washed, paintings unpinned and laid out to dry, drawing boards stacked against the wall. Ah! There's the bell! Front row first, Timothy leading, then Robin, in single file – go!'

John, alone, walked slowly in the throng hurrying past him along the corridors to the school cafeteria.

The school was proud of its cafeteria and the food served in it. The room was spacious and light, with windows all the way along one side overlooking the playground and the playing field beyond. The opposite side was taken up entirely by the shiny silver service counter.

Several boys and girls were already settled at tables by the time John took his place in the queue. Enviously he watched a boy at a

nearby table suck at straws dipped in a milk bottle that was dull with cold. John could imagine the refreshing taste of the well-chilled creamy milk. At another table a group of girls were eating red cherries. John could almost feel the firm fruit on his tongue and the pleasure of biting through the tart, juicy pulp. The cherries must be delicious — and thirst-quenching!

John unhappily took a tray from the pile and slid it along the rails in front of the top of the counter. He put a paper napkin, a glass and a gleaming spoon, a knife and a fork on the tray. It seemed hardly worth while, but he felt that he might as well *try* the food and drink.

'Perhaps,' he muttered to himself, 'if I eat a different way, if I don't let anything touch my lips, my lunch won't all change into chocolate.' But he was not very hopeful.

'What?' asked the boy standing behind him.

'Nothing,' John said.

'I thought I heard you say something about chocolate,' the boy said. 'I hope this is a day for choclate-cream pie. That'd be super.'

On chocolate-cream pie days of the past, John had been know to skip the main course, so that he could spend all his lunch money on dessert. The thought of four pieces of chocolate-cream pie now suddenly made his stomach feel as though he were plunging up and down in the Ghost Train at some night-mare amusement park – an uneasy, flibberty-jibberty sensation. John shuddered and wrinkled his nose.

'Ee-yuk!' he exclaimed.

The other boy shrugged his shoulders and began choosing his meal.

John selected a plate of cold chicken and ham, potato crisps and a lettuce-and-tomato salad. The white of the chicken, the pink of the ham, the gold of the potatoes, the pale green of the lettuce and the red of the tomato were extremely appetizing. He also took half a pint of milk, a thick-crusted whole-wheat roll of bread and a cool pat of butter, a tumbler of water with ice cubes clinking against the glass and a dish of fresh fruit — slices of orange and grapefruit and banana and apple and grapes.

John's tray was loaded with exactly the sort of meal his mother was always trying to persuade him to eat. Until today, John had always thought that 'sensible things' were pretty dull. Today they looked marvellous, and his mouth began to water in its new sticky way.

He paid for the lunch with the money his mother had given him, went to an empty table and sat down.

His fingers were trembling slightly with nervousness as he cut a slice of lettuce. His fork went through the leaves with a promising crunch. He stuck the prongs of the fork into a mouth-sized piece of lettuce and carefully inserted it into his mouth. The lettuce did not touch his wide-stretched lips. John's teeth came together in layers of sweet chocolate.

He took a small piece of potato crisp,

tilted back his head until he was looking up at the ceiling, and dropped the morsel straight down into his throat. He felt it go down, a sharp fragment of sweet chocolate. He tried the milk, the ice-water, the fruit. Every solid and liquid that he sampled was transformed into chocolate as soon as it entered his mouth.

Then he became aware of a shocking novelty that he had not noticed at breakfast. At the rim of each glass there was a small semicircle of opaque brown; the bowl of his spoon and the prongs of his fork had become brown. As John watched, horrified, the areas of magic chocolate slowly spread, until at last the glasses and cutlery were all solid chocolate. The trouble was unquestionably growing worse.

John's scalp tightened with fear.

'What am I going to do?' he asked himself miserably. 'Oh, dear, oh, dear! What is going to happen to me?'

Leaving his tray of chocolate food and drink and utensils, John stumbled away from the cafeteria and out to the playground.

Eight

English passed without incident. Miss Plimsole distributed word lists for her pupils to take home.

'Make sure you learn how to spell them correctly,' she said, as always. 'The more words you know, the more exactly you can think.'

John noticed some difficult new words, including *avarice, indigestion, moderation* and *digestibility*. As Miss Plimsole explained the meaning of each one, it seemed to John that all of them had a special bearing on his present uncomfortable condition.

At last the bell rang.

'Very well, class,' Miss Plimsole said. 'Time for outside activities. Good afternoon.'

'Good afternoon, Miss Plimsole.'

Susan played a violin in the school orchestra, and usually she and John went to the rehearsals in the auditorium together. This time Susan hurried ahead of him. John followed very slowly.

The members of the orchestra were sitting at their music stands on the stage when John, carrying his dark-blue trumpet case, got to his chair in the brass section. Mrs Quaver had already begun to explain a difficult passage to the girl who played the flute.

'Just after Jay sings, " . . . nestlings chirp and flee," Mrs Quaver was saying, 'you come in with your trill – *doodle-oodle-oodle-oo*. Do you see the place on your score? Good.'

'Ah, John,' she said, seeing him in his place. 'I'm glad you're not absent. As I have told the others, this afternoon we're having the first joint rehearsal of my arrangement of "A Boy's Song," by James Hogg. We have been over all the individual parts and all the sections. Now it's time to fit the pieces together.'

John nervously opened his trumpet case and took his shining golden trumpet from its bed of scarlet velvet. The beautiful new instrument gave him confidence. He worked the valves nimbly with his fingers and looked up again at Mrs Quaver.

'Now, John,' she said, 'tell me when your

little solo begins.'

'Right after the end of the second verse,' he promptly replied. He had practised his part every evening in the basement at home for the past two weeks. He knew every note perfectly, by heart. 'After the line, "*That's the way for Billy and me*".'

'Very good,' Mrs Quaver said. 'And don't forget what I told you, John. This is a *happy* song. I want you to play it *happily* – *tah*-tuh, *tah*-tuh, *tah*-tuh-tuh, *ta-a-ah*, simply repeating the rhythm of the voice. And I want you

to be *light* and *lively*. This is the song of a boy who loves romping in the country.'

Tah-tuh, *tah*-tuh, *tah*-tuh-tuh, *ta-a-ah*, John thought. That shouldn't be too difficult, even with the whole orchestra listening to him. He had played it over and over again at home. But he would have to try extra hard here. This was to be his first solo. Everyone else was depending on him to play it properly.

'All right then,' Mrs Quaver said with a merry twinkle in her eyes. With her baton, she rapped twice sharply on the music stand in front of her. All the musicians brought their instruments into playing positions. Susan poised her bow over the strings of her violin. John held his trumpet close to his mouth and wiggled his fingers on the valves.

Mrs Quaver's baton moved from side to side, up, and then down! The cymbals clashed and the drums thumped. The pianist brought his fingers down on the ivory keys of the piano. The violinists and 'cellists made their wheeing and whumping sounds. All were in perfect unison. The rehearsal had begun.

After the introduction, one of the older boys began to sing:

62

> '*Where the pools are bright and deep,*
> *Where the grey trout lies asleep,*
> *Up the river and over the lea,*
> *That's the way for Billy and me.*'

After the last line of the first verse, John's fellow trumpeter echoed the rhythm of the singer —'*Tah*-tuh, *tah*-tuh, *tah*-tuh-tuh, *ta-a-ah*!'

Mrs Quaver smiled approvingly at the successful performance and, with her baton, gave the singer the signal to begin the second verse.

> '*Where the blackbird sings the latest,*'
> (an oboe went *peep*)
> '*Where the hawthorn blooms the sweetest,*
> *Where the nestlings chirp and flee,*'
> (the flute warbled according to plan)
> '*That's the way for Billy and me-e-e!*'

John swallowed, though he had nothing to swallow, and put the mouthpiece of the trumpet to his lips for his solo. The mouthpiece instantly changed into chocolate. Then the chocolate rapidly spread along the instrument, changing all the shiny gold into dull brown.

The first note came out fairly true – '*Tah-*'

– but chocolate trumpets cannot withstand much pressure. The hole in the mouthpiece softened and clogged up, and the valves stuck as John desperately tried to finish his part. Mrs Quaver's eyes almost popped out of her head as she listened to him try to play:

'tuh,
    too-
        tuh,
            ter-t-t
               t-t
                 t-'

It sounded as if John were trying to play a soap-filled bubble-pipe. Terribly flustered, he put down his trumpet.

Mrs Quaver was speechless. The orchestra rocked with uproarious laughter. The other trumpeter leaned over towards John's chair and picked up the trumpet.

'It's a chocolate trumpet!' the boy shouted. 'No wonder it sounded so weird! John Midas was trying to play a chocolate trumpet!'

John did not wait to hear any more. He fled from the stage and out to the playground. Without stopping even to look around, he ran through the stone gateway and homeward.

Nine

Oh, the shame of it! The humiliation! John wept breathlessly as he ran, shocked and frightened and angry at the world that had turned against him.

Mean old things, he thought, blaming Miss Plimsole and Mrs Quaver, even though nothing that had happened had really been their fault.

Horrible old school, he thought, though he had liked school until that morning.

Hateful Susan, he thought, though he was really longing for her to be friendly again.

Mrs Midas, looking out through the window, saw John coming up the pathway.

'Hello, John!' she called from the living room. 'You're home early,' she said, opening the front door. 'How nice! As a reward, there'll be a piece of chocolate after your tea.'

'I hate it!' John shouted. He was crying too hard to say anything else for a moment.

'What's the matter, dear?' Mrs Midas asked, putting her arm around him. He twisted away from her grasp, ran past her, and started up the stairs.

'Susan doesn't want me at her birthday party,' he said as he went. 'Well, I don't want to go to her rotten old party, anyway!'

'I'm sure you don't mean that,' Mrs Midas said. 'Besides,' she added, and John was halted by the softness of her voice, 'Mrs Buttercup telephoned to say she's driving over at four o'clock to pick you up. Come to think of it, you'll only have time for a quick glass of milk.'

'She did?' John said, blinking down at his mother from the stairs.

'Yes, she did,' Mrs Midas assured him. 'So you'd better hurry and get yourself washed and brushed. Your party clothes are laid out on your bed.'

There were games on the Buttercups' lawn while it was still warm enough outside. Later the party supper, including the birthday cake, was going to be served indoors, and there would be a magician and a cartoon film.

John joined in the blind man's buff,

grandmother's footsteps and fox and geese and became quite cheerful. He even forgot about chocolate.

Susan looked very pretty. Her yellow hair was shiny. She was wearing a big blue ribbon the same colour as her eyes. Her cheeks were flushed with excitement – a deeper pink than her new party dress, which had a white collar and white cuffs on its short sleeves. On her feet were dainty little white socks and white shoes with straps which buttoned.

Between games, Susan smiled at John and said: 'I'm glad you came.'

They seemed to be on good terms again.

Then Mr Buttercup approached, bringing a bucket of water from the garage. He set it down in the middle of the lawn without spilling a single drop.

'We're going to duck for apples,' Susan whispered to John. 'The boys against the girls. You can be the captain of the boys' team.'

The two teams lined up for the race. Susan was the captain of the girls.

'The idea is this,' Mr Buttercup said. 'When I say *go* – not yet, John! – Susan and John will race to the bucket. There are twelve apples floating in the water in the bucket and twelve children in the race. Using only their teeth, Susan and John will grab their apples and run back. As soon as they touch the hands of the Number Two runners they'll run to duck for *their* apples, and so on. Does everybody understand? Right! One to get ready, two to get steady, and three to go!'

Susan bounded ahead and had her face deep in the bucket by the time John reached her side and crouched down for his apple.

He got his eye on a big red one with its stalk jutting up conveniently for him to grab. He lowered his face, opened his mouth, and lunged. Somehow his nose reached the apple before his teeth did and pushed it below the surface of the water. John's mouth followed the apple down.

And then a terrible thing happened. The clear water in the bucket turned into dark-brown, sweet, liquid chocolate. Susan and John immediately pulled their heads up. But

it was too late. Their faces were drenched with chocolate syrup.

'Oh!' Susan exclaimed, wiping chocolate out of her eyes. Chocolate syrup dripped down all over her white collar and her pale-pink dress. 'Oh!' she moaned.

John was in the same state. There was chocolate all over his face. There was chocolate on his white shirt-front and on his grey flannel shorts. And there was chocolate in his mouth.

'Glug!' John spluttered.

Susan was too shocked to speak. For the second time that day, she turned her back on John and ran away from him.

Mrs Buttercup, who couldn't understand what had happened, offered to clean John up. But he couldn't bear to stay at the party for another minute. He started for home.

Ten

Dragging along and thinking of all the dreadful things that had happened, John had walked about half-way home when he heard the cheerful voice of his father.

'Hello, hello!' called Mr Midas, crossing over from the other side of the street. He was on his way home from the station. 'You left the party rather early, didn't you? What on earth?' He had just seen the patches and streaks of chocolate that were drying on John's face and clothes. 'Good gracious!' Mr Midas said. 'No wonder you left early! How did *that* happen?'

John burst into tears. He couldn't help it. Everything had been so awful. But now he could tell his father all about it. He stopped crying and only sniffed a little now and then as he told the whole story – about taking the coin to the sweetshop, about buying the box with only one chocolate in it, about the toothpaste, breakfast, the gloves, Susan's coin, the pencil, lunch, the trumpet and finally the apple-ducking water.

'They all turned into chocolate?' Mr Midas said. 'Are you sure you didn't imagine any of this?'

'Look at me,' John said, as though the chocolate stains were proof.

'Well,' Mr Midas said, frowning doubtfully. 'We're not far from that sweetshop of yours – not that I've ever noticed one there. Suppose we stroll over and ask the man whether his chocolates have ever done strange things to anyone else?'

'The shop's on the next corner,' John said, recognizing some of the houses on the side street. 'Not the next house, not the next,' he said. 'But . . . ' His voice faded into silence.

The corner where he had found the sweetshop was nothing now but a vacant building site – flat, open ground littered with a pile of

rusty tins and broken bottles around a splintery old sign that said FOR SALE.

'Hmmm,' said Mr Midas, with an anxious glance at John. 'I think we'd better pay a visit to Dr Cranium before we go home.'

'That's where the shop was,' John insisted, beginning to cry again. He had shed more tears that day, it seemed, and certainly eaten more chocolate, than in all the other days of his life put together. 'I know it was.'

Dr Cranium was a busy man. But he agreed to see Mr Midas and John almost at once.

'Well, well, well, well, well!' said Dr Cranium. 'And how are we getting along now, John? Have we cut down on our sweets?'

John gloomily looked down at the floor.

'Apparently he's had a bad day, Dr Cranium,' Mr Midas said. 'Trouble at school, you know. And a little accident at a birthday party. What I'm worried about is that he keeps saying that everything he puts into his mouth turns into chocolate.'

'No more than a nursery fantasy, I'm sure,' Dr Cranium said to Mr Midas. 'Well, John,' he went on, looking down with a smile, 'suppose you tell me in your own words what seems to be the matter.'

'Everything I put into my mouth turns into chocolate,' John said. 'I'm thirsty. And I'm getting a pain – a bad one, I think.'

Dr Cranium sighed patiently and invited John to open his mouth and say 'Ah'.

'Ah,' John said.

Dr Cranium peered into John's mouth briefly and gave a low whistle of surprise.

'This chocolate-eating must stop,' he said. He went to a supply cabinet.

'I don't think there's any time to be lost,' he told Mr Midas. 'I'm going to give the boy some of my own special compound – *Dr Cranium's Elixir*, I call it. It never fails.'

Dr Cranium took a large bottle from a crowded shelf. He filled a spoon with an oily, greenish-yellowish medicine.

'It doesn't taste very pleasant,' Dr Cranium admitted. 'But I'm sure it'll do the trick. Clear the stomach and you clear the mind – that's what I always say.'

Dr Cranium offered John the spoon, which was full to the brim.

'Must I?' John asked his father. 'I know it'll turn into chocolate.'

'Go on,' Mr Midas said, nodding encouragingly. 'Drink it down, John.'

John took the spoon between his lips. The

75

medicine turned into chocolate. The spoon turned into chocolate. John choked and coughed and chocolate syrup spurted from his mouth.

Dr Cranium dropped the spoon in alarm. When it struck the white-tiled floor, the chocolate handle snapped into several pieces.

'Mercy!' said Dr Cranium. 'I've never seen anything like it! The boy's whole system seems to be so chocolatified that it chocolatizes everything it touches.' After he had recovered somewhat, the doctor went on. 'I believe that this must be an unprecedented case of . . . er . . . chocolatitis. I shall call it Cranium's Disease. The British Medical Association shall hear of this. I shall write a paper for *The Lancet*. I shall want to make an exhaustive study of the child. I –'

'I think John has had enough excitement for one day,' Mr Midas said, interrupting him.

Eleven

Mrs Midas was upset when Mr Midas told her that John had Cranium's Disease.

'He said it was chocolatitis,' Mr Midas said, frowning more deeply than ever. 'But he's calling it Cranium's Disease, because it was his discovery.'

'Dr Cranium didn't do it,' John said. 'It's magic. It all started when I ate that chocolate. I'm scared.'

Mrs Midas sat down and dabbed at her eyes with a lace handkerchief. She was crying.

Mr Midas blew his nose, said he had to attend to something and abruptly left the room.

John had been so busy feeling sorry for himself that he had not realised how his mother and father would feel about his chocolate disease.

'Never mind, Mummy,' he said, putting an arm around her shoulders. 'It's all right.'

Really nothing was all right, but he couldn't

bear to see his mother's tears. He kissed her
wet cheek. His eyes were shut as his lips
softly touched her. Then his lips felt sticky.
He opened his eyes. His mother had turned
into a lifeless statue of chocolate!

John ran wildly out of the house without
thinking where he was going or what he was
going to do. All he knew was that somehow
he must get help. For the first time in a long
while he forgot about himself. Now he didn't

care about anything but bringing his mother back to life.

Without quite knowing how he got there, he found himself at the corner where he had bought the magic chocolate. The building site was not vacant now. The sweetshop was where it had been before. But the displays of sweets no longer occupied the show windows. In one of them there were a chocolate trumpet, a chocolate pencil, and a coin with a piece bitten out of it. In the other there were chocolate utensils on a cafeteria tray and the remains of a chocolate lunch. Evidently, the proprietor of the shop must know a lot about John's hateful chocolate touch. John rushed into the shop.

The proprietor was standing behind the counter carefully polishing something small and round and flat and silver.

'I was just thinking about you,' he said.

John had no time to waste on pleasantries.

'Remember-the-coin-I-found-and-gave-you-for-the-magic-chocolate?' he demanded. Without waiting for a reply, he babbled on: 'I-ate-it-and-it-made-everything-that-touches-my-mouth-turn-into-chocolate-and-I-kissed-my-mother-and-now-she's-chocolate-and-I've-got-to-change-her-back!'

'Easy now,' murmured the shopkeeper. 'Calm down.' There was an expression of satisfaction in the old man's eyes.

'It's all your fault!' John declared.

'My goodness!' the shopkeeper exclaimed. 'Whose fault, did you say?'

'Yours! If you hadn't sold me that chocolate –'

'Now, John,' the shopkeeper interrupted in a gentle but firm voice, 'if you'll be truthful, perhaps I can help you.'

John's ears reddened. It was becoming increasingly apparent to him that he had only himself to blame for all his unhappiness. He looked straight into the shopkeeper's eyes.

'I'll do anything,' John said. 'I'll work for you all my life for nothing, if you'll bring my mother back to life. You can turn me into chocolate, instead, if you want. You –'

'Good,' the shopkeeper said. 'So if you had to choose between restoring your mother to life and getting rid of the chocolate touch, which would it be?'

For a moment, John couldn't help imagining a future of all-chocolate meals. The thought was terrible. But then he thought of his mother as he had left her, a motionless chocolate statue, unable to speak, her chocolate hand still holding her lace handkerchief. Without any further hesitation, John said: 'Help my mother!'

'Well, John,' the shopkeeper said, 'I'm going to give you another chance. When you go to school your pencil will be a real wooden pencil with lead in it.'

'But –' John began to protest. What did the pencil matter?

'The chocolate knife and fork and spoon you left on your tray in the cafeteria will have turned back into metal. Your glass will be glass. Your chocolate trumpet will be a shiny golden one again.'

'But –' John said.

'Don't worry about Dr Cranium's spoon,' the shopkeeper continued smoothly. 'He will find a whole silver one on the floor, where the broken chocolate one lay.'

'But how about – ?'

'Susan Buttercup will discover that the chocolate stains on her party dress and her party shoes were nothing but water, after all. Her coin will be restored to silver wholeness.'

John could stand the suspense no longer.

'My mother!' he shouted. 'What about her? Will *she* be all right?'

The shopkeeper smiled.

'Why don't you run along home and find out?' he suggested.

John turned without even saying goodbye and ran from the shop.

The shopkeeper went back to the task of polishing. The coin had to be polished smooth, ready for a new face and a new set of initials in case anybody needed them.

Twelve

The front door was open. John ran into the living room, where he had left his mother.

She was not there, but on the chair was a small, wet lace handkerchief.

John ran into the dining room and on to the kitchen. As he came to the kitchen door, he heard the ring of silver against crockery. Then he saw a wonderful sight – his mother arranging the tea things on a tray!

He dashed into the kitchen and flung his arms around his mother's waist, sobbing and laughing with relief and joy.

'There, there,' said Mrs Midas, stroking the hair from John's forehead. 'You've had a very disturbing day, dear. Goodness! I'm really looking forward to a cup of tea, myself. I felt quite strange just then in the other room. I don't know what came over me.'

The door from the garden opened and Mr Midas came in.

'Before we sit down,' Mrs Midas said to John, 'have a glass of cold milk. You look so hot.'

So they didn't know what had happened to her! John certainly wasn't going to frighten them by telling them. He watched gratefully as his mother took a frosty blue jug from the refrigerator and poured from it a glassful of ice-cold creamy milk.

Trembling with nervousness, John tilted the glass against his open mouth. The liquid flowed in and down his throat – and remained purely milky, deliciously milky, tasting of nothing but fresh milk! After the first long, wonderful gulps, he suddenly realised that he had not thanked the shopkeeper for saving John's mother.

'Mummy,' John said, 'please may I go out for a minute. I'll be right back.'

'All right, John,' she said. 'But don't be long. We're going to have an early supper.'

John ran down the street until he came to the corner where he usually turned right when he was going to Susan's house. There he turned left, along the street that had taken him to the sweetshop.

But there was no sweetshop.

On the corner there was only a heap of

rusty tins and broken bottles around a signboard with new lettering, which said –
SOLD.